JACE

WOLVES OF THE RISING SUN #1

KENZIE COX

Published by Bayou Moon Press, LLC, 2015.

This is a work of fiction. Similarities to real people, places, or events are entirely coincidental.

Jace: WOLVES OF THE RISING SUN #1
First edition.

JOIN THE PACKS OF THE MATING SEASON

The mating moon is rising…

Wherever that silver light touches, lone male werewolves are seized by the urge to find their mates. Join these six packs of growly alpha males (with six-packs!) as they seek out the smart, sassy women who are strong enough to claim them forever.

The "Mating Season" werewolf shifter novellas are brought to you by six authors following the adventures of six different packs. Each novella is the story of a mated pair (or trio!) with their Happily Ever After. Enjoy the run!

Learn more at thematingseason.com

JACE: WOLVES OF THE RISING SUN

In the wilds of the bayou…

Jace Riveaux has wanted her since the first moment she stepped into his bayou bar three years ago. And now she's back, unattached, and ready for the taking. One afternoon together, and he knows she's the one. Only his world is dangerous, he has secrets, and trust is hard to come by…especially when all signs point to her being aligned with his enemy.

Skye Michaels has nothing left to lose. After a bad breakup, she flees to her favorite southern Louisiana town, determined to finally get photographs of the majestic wolves that roam the area. Instead she gets what she really came for—Jace Riveaux. But when the Riveauxs are threatened by someone she knows, suddenly she has more to lose than ever.

Sign up for Kenzie's newsletter here at www.kenziecox.com. Do you prefer text messages? Sign up for text alerts! Just text SHIFTERSROCK to 24587 to register.

CHAPTER 1

SKYE

Everything about the shack known as Wolves of the Rising Sun was shabby except the shirtless man pouring shots behind the bar. God, was he beautiful. Wide shoulders, narrow waist, dark wavy hair that fell to his chin. Vibrant ink covered both arms and a stylized wolf symbol was tattooed over his heart. I was too far away to make out the details, but I'd seen it before and knew it was the same as the one outside on the marquee.

I practically drooled standing there in the

doorway.

Snap out of it, Skye. The last thing you need is another man in your life. Even if that man is Jace Riveaux.

Clutching my camera case, I sucked in a breath and strolled up to the rough-hewn bar, flashing the secret smile I reserved just for him. What can I say? Even though I wasn't looking for a date, I couldn't pass up an opportunity to flirt with the guy I'd had a crush on for the past two years.

Jace didn't disappoint. He shoved one of the shots he'd just poured toward his brother Aiden, an equally drool-worthy male, and then turned to me, his eyes glittering with what I could only call trouble. "Well, look who it is. Skye Michaels." He leaned over the bar toward me. "What's brought your pretty little self all the way out here to my bayou?"

Little? Oh, he'd doubled his tip already. I fought back the urge to lick my lips and smiled. "Right this minute, all I'm hoping for is something to quench this thirst."

It was early March, and even though it wasn't technically spring yet, the higher-than-normal temperatures combined with the broken air conditioner in my old Jeep had taken it out of me.

"What's your poison?" He waved at the bottles behind him, a challenge in his grin. "Tequila? Whiskey? Jäger?"

I gave him a look of mock horror and chuckled. "Not if I'm going to walk out of here sometime today. How about a margarita? On the rocks. The good tequila." I nodded toward the row of fancy bottles off to the left. "Anything one hundred percent agave."

His brow rose in curious respect. "Coming right up." He turned and his shoulder muscles rippled with the movement.

Lordy. My girl parts tingled just watching him.

"Here for a photo shoot?" Aiden asked, eyeing my camera case.

I turned and smiled at him, wistfully wishing I had been blessed with his dark blond hair. He already had natural, sun-lightened streaks from the Southern sun. "Of course. What else would I be up to?"

He glanced at my pack and back at the Nikon hanging at my waist. "Let's see. I don't know. How about finally putting my brother out of his misery and shagging him already?"

"Aiden," Jace growled from across the bar.

Heat crawled up my neck, and I had to force myself to not look at Jace. If I did, he'd see right through me. Know I wanted him. Always had. Only up until two days ago, I'd had a boyfriend. Now I didn't. But Jace didn't know that. Not yet anyway. Maybe not ever, since I was going to die from embarrassment.

Downing his shot, Aiden slammed the glass back on the bar and grinned at me, his green eyes dancing with amusement. "Come on, Jace. Everyone knows you two are hot for each other. Why don't you just get it on already? Honestly, it's getting uncomfortable to watch."

"Give it a rest. You're embarrassing yourself," Jace said.

From the corner of my eye, I saw Jace turn his back on us as he continued making my drink.

"If you say so, brother." Aiden turned to face me, a lock of his hair falling over one eye. "Who's taking you out into the bayou this time? I didn't see anything on the schedule."

I bit my lip. No one goes out into the bayou without a guide. Usually I called ahead and booked an airboat so I could get shots way out in the areas that remained untouched, but I hadn't even known until a few hours ago that I was going to come here. To say it had been a spur-of-the-moment thing would be an understatement. "I forgot to make an appointment. Is there anyone free? If not, I can wait. I'm planning to stay down here for a few days at least. Maybe longer."

Aiden arched his eyebrows in surprise. "Well, isn't that interesting." Then he laughed. "Jace is busy tending bar, but you're in luck. I happen to have some free time today. As soon as you've finished that drink, I can take you for a spin."

A faint trace of disappointment settled in my chest. I liked Aiden, and it was true I'd had a thing for Jace forever, but more importantly, Jace was a real friend. And I needed one more than ever right then. After what had happened with my ex... All I wanted was a friendly shoulder to lean on. Aiden would flirt and tease me into exasperation. "We don't have to if you're busy. I can hang out here until dusk and then set up for some sunset shots over the river."

"Sunsets. Right." Aiden shook his head. "We all know you'd be waiting for the wolves."

"I—"

"Forget it. It's dangerous," Jace said, setting

my drink in front of me.

I lifted my gaze and stared into his dark eyes. The truth was I couldn't care less about the bayou shots. In addition to seeing Jace, I had come for the wolves. Had been thinking of them all the way down from Baton Rouge. Catching their majestic beauty and grace in a photo had become an obsession of mine ever since I'd first caught a glimpse of the pack two years ago right outside the bar. "Have you seen any of them lately?"

His eyes narrowed and a muscle pulsed in his jaw. "No, Skye. And don't even think of wondering off to go look for them. Last time you did that—"

I held up a hand, stopping him. "Okay. Got it. But you're not going to stop me from getting my sunset shots are you?"

He gave me a flat stare. "No. Not as long as you stay on the property."

"Fine." I pushed the straw around in my margarita just for something to focus on. Jace was right to be cautious of course. Six months ago, I'd wandered out into the woods with my camera and had gotten lost because I hadn't been paying attention. Luckily, Jace had found me. In the dark. At two a.m. Talk about embarrassing.

I'd been fine, but damn, the bayou is scary at night. And Jace had been really upset. After he'd carried me out, he'd yelled at me for five minutes straight. When he was done, he'd hugged me hard enough to knock the wind out of me. I'd decided it'd been worth it.

"Drink up," Aiden said. "It's fixin' to storm before long. If you want to get out on the water and back without getting drenched, we'll need to go soon."

"You're not going anywhere, *brother*," Jace said, mocking him.

Aiden's head snapped up as he stared at his brother in bemusement. "Why? You afraid I'm going to steal her from you? I could, you know. All I'd have to do is—"

"The supply order needs to be placed within the hour. Did you get the inventory done?"

"Shit." Aiden took a pull from his longneck beer bottle. "Sorry, sweetheart. Work calls. Looks like you're going to have to wait it out while I do the grunt work for that one." He nodded at Jace. "Lazy bastard."

Jace wiped the bar down and then threw the rag under the counter. "Let's go, Skye. I need to check on something at the cabin anyway."

Both Aiden and I turned, giving him our full attention. My pulse sped up. Alone with Jace. At the cabin. Holy crap. I wasn't ready for this. Well, maybe…

Aiden let out a whoop of laughter. "Looks like all that denial was bullshit. Careful, sweetheart. It *is* mating season. Beware if he tries to bite—"

"Aiden," Jace barked. "Shut up."

"What?" Aiden asked with an air of mock innocence.

Jace strode out from behind the counter and placed his hand on the small of my back. A tingle shot up my spine, and I shivered.

"Everything okay?" Jace asked.

"Air-conditioning," I said by way of explanation.

He nodded and then turned to Aiden.

"We're going to take a quick ride out to the island. Try not to offend anyone while we're gone."

"Sure. Whatever you say." Aiden glanced at me and then smirked at Jace. "But you know I'm right. And when it happens, you owe me a week off and a bottle of single malt. The expensive shit. Not that stuff you keep behind the bar." Aiden nodded to me. "Have fun."

"I always do."

Aiden snorted and strode from the bar area into the back, his movements powerful and full of grace. I had no trouble imagining him wrestling a five-hundred-pound gator and winning. Now that would be something to see.

"You ready to go?" Jace asked, completely ignoring his brother's outburst.

"What was he talking about?" I asked, certain it had something to do with me.

Gazing down at me, he met my eyes and my stomach did a little flip at the interest I saw shining back at me. Holy crap. It was too effing hot in here. He was too effing hot.

He tore his gaze away and cleared his throat. "We better get going."

"Yeah. Okay." I clutched my camera case, desperate for something else to focus on. "If you're sure you can spare the time."

"Aiden's got it under control." He jerked his head, inviting me outside.

I stepped back into the oppressive heat and stood on the weathered wooden porch. "Since when is it ever this hot in March?"

He shook his head. "Heat wave." Then his gaze traveled the length of my body, lingering on my bare legs.

I'd chosen a pale yellow sundress that hit a few inches above my knee, but the way he was devouring me with his intense gaze, I was starting to feel like I was wearing nothing but my Victoria's Secret lace. "Umm…"

He raised his gaze to meet mine, a secret smile claiming his lips. "It was my turn."

I pulled my camera from its case and frowned at him. "Your turn for what?"

His smile reached his eyes. "You took your time checking me out. Twice. Don't think I didn't notice. So I did the same. Only I didn't ask you to take your shirt off… yet."

Whoa. My pulse thudded in my throat. As a former plus-sized model, I was used to that sort of attention, but not from him. At least not that blatant. Like he wanted to press me up against the side of the building and take me right there, dress or no. I swallowed the nervousness threatening to choke me. "And?"

"And what?"

I cast a quick glance down my body. "Did I pass inspection?"

Oh, God. Why did I just say that? Flirting wasn't supposed to be on the menu this trip. In fact, I'd sworn off men somewhere about an hour outside Baton Rouge.

His dark eyes turned molten, and I half expected him to check me out again. But instead he took a step toward me, invading my personal space.

I sucked in a breath. He smelled faintly of soap and fresh-cut grass. Like he'd just cleaned up after working in the yard.

He leaned in and his breath tickled my ear. "In order to answer your question, I'd need a closer look."

"Jace!" I laughed to cover my surprise and wrapped my arms around myself to stop the shiver of desire. What had gotten into him? I expected that sort of talk from Aiden, but Jace was usually much more subtle.

He leaned against the railing, his feet crossed at the ankle, watching me.

After a moment of silence, I cleared my throat. "Anyway. I think I'd like some shots from the shore. If you have anything you need to do, don't let me stop you."

"Seriously? I don't mind taking you out on the boat."

I nodded, not trusting myself to speak. He'd thrown me off guard. And I needed some time to regroup before I was trapped on a boat with him.

"All right, then. I'll be over there if you need anything." He nodded toward a shed behind the bar.

"Thanks, but I'm sure I'll be fine." I strode down the worn dirt path toward the river, my fingers cramping from the death grip I had on the camera strap.

"You already are," I heard him mumble behind me.

An uncontrollable smile tugged at my lips as I adjusted the settings on my camera. Glancing over my shoulder, I caught him disappearing into a shed. Too bad. If I hadn't wanted to avoid dying from embarrassment, I would've loved to get him into a few of the shots. Hell, who was I kidding? I'd spend the entire week staring at him through the viewfinder if I had my way. But Jace hated having his picture taken. Anytime I pointed the camera in his direction, he bolted. It was damned frustrating.

Sighing, I turned and strode onto the dock, doing my best to put Jace, the bar, and everything except the low layer of fog clinging to the river out of my mind.

CHAPTER 2

JACE

THE AXE SLICED through the cypress wood with a satisfying thud. The mild ache in my muscles served as a reminder that I'd spent too much time indoors lately. Spent entirely too much time serving the fishermen of southeast Louisiana instead of searching for a mate to strengthen the pack.

Damn Aiden, bringing up mating season in front of Skye. What the hell was he up to? She knew wolves roamed our area, but she had no idea *we* were the wolves and that we were shifters. And I intended to keep it that way. There was no denying I was fiercely attracted to her, had wanted her from the moment I'd first met her, but I'd been involved with someone else. And now she had a serious boyfriend. The live-in kind. Some jackass who'd lost his trust fund money in risky business investments. Or so I'd been told after she'd had one too many beers last fall.

No, Skye was completely off-limits. Even if it killed me to stay away from her. I was certain if she kept hanging out here, one day my brothers would be digging my grave. Because I was going out of my mind wanting her.

Balancing another log, I blew out a breath and slammed the door on that thought. Even if she weren't attached, the last thing I needed was a repeat of the previous season. The memory of waking up to an empty bed and a half-empty closet swam in my mind.

"Fuck." I tightened my grip on the axe and swung. The blade sliced through the wood and the two halves fell with a solid thunk.

"Jace?"

I twisted to find the golden-haired photographer near the large cypress, holding her camera with both hands. Her creamy skin and pink cheeks practically glowed in the sunshine. Fucking gorgeous. I raised one eyebrow. "Done already?"

"Um, no." She cast a quick glance toward the dock and gave me a tentative smile. "I was wondering if it would be too much trouble to take me down the river just a bit. I'm trying to get a specific shot and I can't quite get it from the shore."

It was always during these moments, when we were alone and her shyness all but overtook her, that the warning bells went off in my head.

Go back into the bar. Tell her to ask Aiden. Stay away.

I very carefully and deliberately leaned the axe against the metal siding of the shed and ignored all reason. Whatever Skye wanted, I was going to give it to her. God knew her douche bag of a boyfriend never did. "Sure."

Her shy smile blossomed. "Thanks for this. I thought I could wait until tomorrow, but with the light and the way the fog is clinging to the water, it's too good to pass up."

"Not a problem." I stepped into the shed and grabbed the key to the boat. When I returned, Skye was lying flat on the dock on her stomach, her eye pressed to the viewfinder of her camera. The faint click, click, click of the button filled the silence.

I stood there, transfixed by her intensity, the passion for her art. Damn, that was sexy. And I wasn't talking about the way her skirt was inching up the back of her shapely legs.

A ripple in the water snapped me out of my trance. "Skye!"

"Hmm?" She didn't budge from her spot.

I grabbed Skye around the waist and hauled her off the dock just before a gator popped out of the water, her large jaws snapping right where Skye's head had been.

"Oh my God!" She gasped, her eyes wide with fear. "I thought the gators around here were docile."

I cradled her against my chest, swallowing my heart trying to clog my throat. "They usually are, but Betsy, she's kinda used to us feeding her from the dock. Your movement drew her out. She thought it was time for lunch."

"Oh."

She stared up at me, and I was certain her deep blue eyes were seeing far more than I wanted them to. Her photographer's eyes. Unease rippled through me, and the moment turned awkward. Setting her on her feet, I took two steps back and directed my gaze back to the water. The large gator had disappeared. "Ready for that ride in the boat?"

"Uh, yeah. I guess." She studied her camera as if to make sure it hadn't been harmed. Then she stood there frozen, her eyes locked on the rippling water.

I gently pried the camera from her, tucked one of her hands in mine, and guided her toward the boat. "Relax. Betsy's gone now. You're perfectly safe."

"I know. It just rattled me is all. I mean, I know gators are here. I've seen them a million times. But none have ever come after me."

The hint of fear in her eyes mixed with her air of innocence sent my pulse racing. She was too sweet to be here like this with me. It was too dangerous for both of us. After holding her in my arms, I could only think of one thing. Getting her out of that dress and under me as fast as possible. If I had even a shred of decency, I'd haul her back to her Jeep and send her on her way. Back to her douche nozzle of a boyfriend. Instead, I nodded toward the water. "Come on."

"You're sure?" she asked, her eyes narrowing as she scanned the now-still water as if she expected the gator to jump up from out of nowhere.

"Positive." I gestured for her to step onto the boat. It was the one we took out for smaller groups, with only two bench seats and a place for the driver. "Gators can't sneak up on us. We'd see her. The only reason you were startled is because you were so focused on whatever shot you were trying to get. She's gone now. I promise."

She hastily made her way onto the boat and perched on the middle of the seat in the second row, her shoulders stiff. I could hardly blame her after that incident. My blood would be racing too if Betsy came after me.

After untying the rope, I stepped into the boat. "There's ear protection under your seat if it's too loud," I said as if she hadn't been on one of these tours a dozen times already.

She shook her head and held her hand out for her camera.

I gave it back to her, sat in the driver's seat at the back of the boat, and asked, "Where to, princess?"

Skye turned around, glaring at me. "Please don't call me that."

Whoa. Where had that come from? Skye never snapped at anyone. Someone in her past had really done a number on her with that pet name. I dropped the smile and nodded. "You got it."

"Thanks." The tension in her shoulders eased. "Can you take us about twenty yards that way through the tree canopy?" She pointed downriver.

"Sure." I fired up the boat and eased out into the river, inching into the envelope of the trees.

Only a few moments had gone by before Skye stood up and got lost in her shots as we meandered along. The low-lying fog still clinging to the river was an eerie contrast to the tree canopy, and I could see why she was so keen to get the shots. The effect was mesmerizing and didn't happen often.

More than thirty minutes went by while Skye took shot after shot from almost every angle possible. I was certain she'd forgotten all about me, but then she turned suddenly and said, "Stop right here."

After killing the motor, I sat back and propped my feet up on the seat in front of me.

"Thanks." She moved to the very front of the boat, snapping photos of the small family cemetery on the other side of the river. It was old and full of raised tombs. Moss hung from the trees, and the way steam rose from the river, it was no surprise she'd asked me to stop. Sun streamed down on the cemetery, and I had no doubt the shots would be stunning. The bayou was beautiful in its harsh reality.

"You're so quiet," she said without turning to look at me.

"I'm just taking in the view."

Skye glanced over her shoulder and caught me staring at her.

Chuckling, she pointed her camera at me. The click of the shutter rang in my ears as I fought to keep the scowl off my face. I didn't do pictures. No shifter did.

"Look." I nodded toward the shoreline.

She turned again, scanning the area.

"They're about three feet to the right of the cemetery," I said quietly.

It took her a second, and then she let out a small gasp. "Baby gators."

Three alligators, each about twelve inches long, lay sunning themselves on a log.

"They're adorable." Click. Click. Click.

"Do you want to go farther out? I have time," I said, pleased with her reaction.

"Well…" She turned in a slow circle.

I saw the moment it happened, when the majestic beauty of the bayou invaded her soul once again. It always did and was part of the reason she always came back here. It pleased me more than it should. It didn't matter that she was affected by this place. She wouldn't stay. She never did, regardless of how much she loved it.

"Yes." She sat back down on the bench and draped her arm over the seat, watching me.

"Hold on." I winked, and before I could talk myself out of it, I restarted the engine and took off toward my secret hiding spot. A place I'd never taken her before.

Five minutes later, we glided into a small, open body of water.

Her eyes widened in delighted surprise, and she made a cutting motion near her neck.

Once again I killed the engine.

"It's gorgeous." She eyed me as she tied her long blond locks up into a haphazard bun.

I glanced down at my chest and back at her, raising one eyebrow.

She laughed. "No, not that." Jerking her head to the right, she said, "The camp. It's perfect. Old wooden porch, peeling paint, jasmine climbing up the side of the house. All it needs is a bottle of moonshine between those rocking chairs."

"A real Cajun never leaves his moonshine unattended."

"No doubt." She glanced at the cabin once more. "Can we get closer?"

I nodded and maneuvered the boat toward the old dock. But just before we got there, a loud boom rumbled overhead. Shit. I'd forgotten all about the impending storm. Glancing up at the rapidly darkening sky, I made a split-second decision. "We have to get out of this."

Skye glanced up and grimaced. "Yikes. Yeah, better head back."

I shook my head. "No time for that." As soon as I got the words out, fat heavy drops of rain splattered on my head.

"Oh crap." Skye frantically stuffed her camera into her carrying case as I jumped off the boat onto the dock and deftly tied the airboat to the pillars.

"Come on." I held my hand out to her.

Another rumble passed overhead. The sky darkened and the heavens opened up, unleashing a torrent of rain.

Skye didn't hesitate. Her hand slipped into mine, and together we ran the short distance to the porch.

"Wow," she said once we were safely under the overhang. Then she glanced down and gasped.

My entire body hardened at the sight of her round, firm breasts clearly visible through her soaked dress.

She wrapped her arms around herself and

turned her back to me.

Her dress clung to her bottom and legs, leaving nothing to the imagination. Jesus. I forced myself to turn around. If I didn't get her covered up, I was going to have to stand out in the downpour just to cool off.

Unlocking the door, I said, "Let's get inside and dry you off."

"Umm…"

I glanced over my shoulder and immediately regretted it. She was slick with rain and so fucking sexy I could barely control my inner wolf. I cleared my throat. "Better hurry. This is about to get worse."

"Worse than this?" Just as she said the words, more thunder rolled and the sky lit up with a flash of lightning. She jumped and pressed herself against the wall of the cabin, her hand clutched to her chest.

This time I didn't look away. I couldn't. My gaze was trained on the drops of water trailing down her chest and into her cleavage. I stood in the threshold, my hand clutching the doorknob, tension rippling through me. Her chest rose and fell with her rapid breathing, taunting me.

"Jace?"

I jerked and met her wide-eyed stare. "Yes?"

"I think we better go inside."

CHAPTER 3

SKYE

THE ONE-ROOM CABIN was spotless. Two leather recliners were positioned in front of a fireplace. Behind the recliners was a simple round table with four mismatched chairs. But what drew my eye was the queen-size bed in the corner made up with a solid navy-blue comforter. This place didn't have a feminine touch anywhere.

The thought pleased me more than it should.

What difference did it make if Jace had a

woman in his life? I wasn't looking for a man, remember? I'd come to the little bayou town to get away from the one living in my former apartment. Shacking up with another one, no matter how gorgeous he was, simply wasn't on the agenda. Or at least it wasn't until he seared me with his heated gaze. Now all I could think about was pushing him down on that bed and—

"Here." Jace pulled a white towel out of a built-in cabinet.

"Thanks." I clutched the towel to my chest and glanced around once more, hoping we hadn't just invaded someone else's space. But Jace did have a key. "Is this your place?"

Nodding, he pulled out another towel and dried his face and chest. "Family property." He draped the towel over the back of a chair and then stood there in his wet jeans, staring out the window at the thunderstorm.

A shiver crept over me as I watched him. The temperature had dropped considerably, but the air was far from chilly. Jace's mere presence was having an uncontrollable effect on me.

Slamming the door on all my recent objections, I dropped the towel and took a step forward, closing the space between us.

He turned and then went completely still. "Skye—"

"Shh." I pressed my finger to his lips and stared up into his dark, smoldering eyes, caving in to the long-suppressed urge to touch him. "I want you."

A voice in the back of my mind screamed at me to take a step back, to put distance between us. This was a mistake. Way too soon after my breakup. But my body was saying something else entirely. And it had been so long since I'd actually been physically attracted to anyone, had given myself to someone who made my heart flutter. I couldn't resist. Didn't even want to.

A hungry look claimed Jace's features. He brought his hands up and slowly ran his fingers over my bare arms. "That's pretty direct there, Skye. Are you sure you want to be saying things like that to me?" He glanced around. "Here in this remote bayou cabin?"

I heard him. Understood what he was saying, but refused to entertain any second-guessing. "I know what I want."

"And that would be?" His lips turned up into a ghost of a smile.

I swallowed and heat burned my cheeks. But I wasn't backing down. Not now. Not when it was clear he wanted me too. I placed my hand on his chest and trailed my fingers down his rigid abs, stopping just above the button of his jeans the way I'd imagined a thousand times before. "I want to wrap my bare legs around you and feel your body pressed up against mine."

His hand slipped down to my hip, his fingers digging into my flesh. His brow furrowed, and I could sense his internal struggle. "Jesus, Skye. What about that boyfriend of yours?"

"We broke up."

Surprise lit his features, followed quickly by a satisfied smile as he tugged me closer. "Is that right?"

I nodded, a tingle of excitement urging me

on. I pressed my lips to the hollow at the base of his throat and tasted his salty skin. I let out a small murmur of satisfaction, loving the way his breathing quickened and his body tightened with clear desire.

"And after you get your gorgeous legs wrapped around me, what then?" he said, his voice hoarse.

I feathered my fingers over his elevated pulse. "I'm going to take you deep inside me and ride you until we both come so hard we forget the rest of the world exists."

Jace stood perfectly still for just a moment. Then a low growl escaped from his lips as he swung me up into his arms and carried me over to the bed. He set me back on my feet and took a step back, his determined expression so intense heat shot to my center.

"Take your dress off," he said, his hands already working the button of his jeans.

I reached out and touched his fingers, stopping him. "Let me."

Reluctantly, he dropped his hands to his sides and stared down at me, his muscles flexing under my touch.

I slowly slid the zipper down on his jeans, letting my knuckles graze his already-hard shaft. God, he was big. And so hard I could barely hold back my own needy growl. I forgot the jeans and took my time, rubbing my palm over his maleness, delighting in the anticipation of him.

"Skye," he said, his tone impatient.

I smiled up at him. "Yes?"

"I've long thought of all the things I'd like to do to you if we ever ended up in this moment. And believe me, I've had a lot of time to get creative. But if you don't move this along, I'm going to lose control and bend you over that table and fuck you hard and fast."

"Oh…" I snatched my hand away and clutched it against my chest. But not because I was shocked at what he'd said. No. His words had lit a molten fire between my thighs, and all I could think about was how he'd feel pressed up against my ass as he pounded into me. I took a deep breath and forced my hand down. I raised one eyebrow, cast a glance at his jeans, and nodded. "Take them off."

His gaze burned into mine as he pulled his jeans off along with his boxer briefs.

I knew he was standing there naked in all his glory, and I was dying to take my fill of his gorgeous body, but I couldn't break away from his lust-filled gaze. All his want and need was right there on the surface, the undeniable craving to finally make me his.

My head swam, and I swayed on my feet, nearly bowled over by the connection we shared. I'd known him for three years and had always been attracted to him. Yet this pull I felt now, it was so much more, so overwhelming and completely new. It was like a switch had been flipped and I couldn't break away.

I could tell he felt it too. He wanted me just as much as I wanted him. Maybe more.

"Your turn," he said. "Take it off. All of it."

My heart raced, thumping against my breastbone so hard it ached. With trembling fingers I slipped the straps off my shoulders, undid the back zipper and let the cotton dress fall to the floor.

His eyes blazed with anticipation for just a moment before he shifted his attention to my breasts. They were spilling out of my favorite pink silk push-up bra, and I congratulated myself on his obvious approval.

"Come here," I said, crooking my finger.

He shook his head. "You're not naked yet."

I smiled. "I thought you might want to finish the job."

"I could, but there won't be much fabric left if you leave it to me."

Holy hotness. I was going to combust right there in the cabin. "Um, okay."

Watching him watch me, I reached around and undid the too-tight bra. He sucked in a breath, his eyes piercing me with his hyperfocused gaze as if he were memorizing every inch of my exposed flesh.

I bit my lip and hooked my thumbs into the elastic of my matching pink lace underwear. Then, closing my eyes, I pulled them down, letting them fall into the circle created by my discarded dress.

"Skye?" Jace's voice was so low and sexy I nearly melted right there.

"Yes?"

"Open your eyes, love. I want to see that gorgeous sapphire blue staring back at me when I touch you for the first time."

My eyes flew open.

He held his hand out and I took it, ready for whatever he had to offer.

Jace twisted me around and tugged me to him so my back was pressed up against his chest. His body molded against mine, his hands clutching my hips as his mouth clamped over the nape of my neck, his teeth teasing and biting.

That shiver came back full force and goose-flesh popped out on my skin. I reached back and clasped my hands over his hard thighs, my head thrown back as I nearly drowned in my need for him. "Touch me everywhere, Jace."

One arm snaked around my waist and he splayed his hand over my stomach, his fingers inching lower, so seductive in his movements.

"Yes," I whispered.

He chuckled and brought the other hand up to cup my breast, his fingers barely squeezing my nipple. "So fucking gorgeous," he said between the biting kisses.

"This is nice, but…"

He froze. "Nice?"

I pressed my ass against his erection, loving

the way he felt against me. "Way better than nice." Peering over my shoulder, I gave him a wicked grin. "But I thought you wanted to see the sapphire in my eyes when you touched me."

He let out a low chuckle. "I had a specific place in mind when I said that."

"You—"

He slipped his hand between my thighs and pressed a finger against my slick heat.

I moaned and my knees went weak. Letting him support me, my eyelids drifted closed as I luxuriated in the sweet ache.

"Open your eyes," he demanded.

I blinked up at him and got caught in the intensity staring back at me. He worked his hand against me, his dark eyes holding mine to him. Everything pulsed. My breasts, my blood, my sex.

"Jace," I said, breathless.

"Shh. I want to watch you come." Two of his fingers slid inside me, and a second later his thumb pressed against my clit.

"Oh, holy… fuck." I gasped and rocked against him. Everything tightened and then suddenly my muscles spasmed. My eyes closed as I clung to him, my fingernails digging into his thighs as the wave crashed through me.

Jace held me tight, his lips nuzzling my neck. I reveled in his attention before I opened my eyes and glanced back at him, biting my lower lip. His gaze locked on my mouth. Time stood still as we both got lost in the moment. But when I released my lip, he swiftly picked me up and laid me gently on the bed.

Kneeling over me, he lowered his head only inches from mine and said, "Those lips have been driving me insane since the moment you walked into the bar three years ago."

I felt the smile spreading, but he cut it off with a searing kiss, his tongue plunging into my mouth, claiming me with his own. He tasted faintly of sugar and cinnamon, and I couldn't get enough. I pulled him down, wanting to feel the weight of him.

"Citrus," he murmured dragging his mouth to my neck.

"Hmm?"

"That's what you taste like. Everywhere."

"It was the margarita," I said, tracing my fingers over the majestic white wolf tattooed on his shoulder.

"It's just you." His head dipped into my cleavage, his tongue darting over my breast until he caught my left nipple between his teeth.

I arched into him and buried one hand in his thick, dark locks. "You're really good at this."

He answered by sucking hard.

I gasped and tilted my pelvis up, wanting him more than ever. "Now, Jace. I need you inside me."

He ignored my plea but cupped my other breast in his large hand, teasing that nipple as well.

All I felt was sensation and need, my nerves on sensory overload. "Jace," I pleaded.

He lifted his head, his eyes glazed with lust.

I cleared my throat and forced out, "Do you have protection?"

He just stared at me for a moment and then shook his head as if to clear the haze from his mind. "Yeah."

"Get it. Now."

His lips turned up into a smug smile.

"I'm waiting."

He dipped his head and nipped at my breast again while one hand reached for the small drawer on the nightstand. He produced a foil wrapper and set it on the pillow beside me.

I grabbed it and pushed him over onto his back. He went willingly and lay patiently, waiting for me to do as I would. But as I ran my hand down his chest, it was painfully obvious he was drowning in his own need. His skin burned with heat, and his muscles quivered under my touch.

Taking my time admiring him, I straddled his legs and leaned down, pressing a trail of kisses down his chest and stomach, stopping only when I got to the tip of his shaft.

"No," he said softly.

I glanced up, lifting an eyebrow in question.

"Not now. I want to be inside you."

That was all I needed to hear. I grabbed the condom and tore it open with my teeth. Then I wrapped my hand around the base of him, loving his velvety feel, and slid the condom on.

"Ride me," he demanded, clutching my hips, his fingers digging into my flesh.

Before I could even move, he lifted me up over himself, pressed into my soft flesh, and then yanked me down, impaling me on his hard cock.

The shock of him made me cry out in a mix of pleasure and pain. "Oh, god," I breathed.

"You okay?" he asked.

I nodded, holding perfectly still as my body adjusted to his intoxicating intrusion.

He loosened his fingers and gently slid them along my inner thighs, teasing the tender flesh. Everything about him felt right. Perfect. And for one insane moment, I had a feeling that this wasn't our first time. That we'd met in another time or place. That we'd been together before.

Jace's hands moved from my thighs to my hips, and he pulled himself up, once again clasping his lips over my nipple. Pleasure shot through me, blocking all my thoughts, and I started to move.

"Yes." Biting gently on my nipple, he flicked his tongue over the hardened peak, making both of my breasts ache.

I quickened my pace, tightening myself around him.

Releasing me, he groaned and fell back onto

the bed, jerking up to match my movements with a fervor of his own.

The small cabin, the thunderstorm, everything around me faded away as I lost myself to the man beneath me. My entire world narrowed and all I knew was him.

CHAPTER 4

JACE

Skye Rose and fell above me, her gorgeous body claiming mine in a way I was certain she didn't understand. Somewhere between that first kiss and our descent to the bed, the afternoon of hot sex with a friend had turned into something far more important... and dangerous for both of us.

Touching her, exploring her luscious body, had brought my wolf right to the surface as I'd known it would. The animal instinct was inherently connected to any type of sexual encounter. But this, the way her touch called up my fierce desire to have every inch of her, to mark her, to claim what was *mine*, was different. I could barely control it. Wanted to flip her over onto her back and drive myself into her over and over again until I lost myself completely and marked her with my wolf bite.

Made her my mate.

The compulsion grew from a tiny seed until it filled my heart and mind, nearly making me come undone with the urgency of it.

"Oh, Jace," Skye said, her voice breathy with passion. "You feel so good."

Her words fueled my fire, and I clamped my hands around her hips, holding her down to me as I ground into her, knowing that I was holding on too tight, that if I couldn't claim her with my bite, I would at least mark her with my touch.

She threw her head back, her lower lip caught between her teeth. She loved it. That much was obvious. With each thrust of my hips, she gasped and clawed at my chest, digging those sharp nails into my skin.

The sting of it chipped away at my self-control, and before I could stop myself, I rolled, flipping us both over, managing to somehow stay joined in her heat.

She let out a breath, staring up at me, her eyes half-lidded with unbridled lust.

I pulled one of her legs higher on my hip, ground my teeth together, and thrust long and hard and deep, filling her completely.

"Yes, Jace. Yes."

She rocked her hips, and I thrust harder and faster, feeling the tightening in my balls as my wolf clawed at the surface, trying to break free.

That undeniable need to make her mine made my mouth water. Just one nip of her tongue and she'd be mine, forced into the shifter life, mated to me… forever.

No! I would not change her without her consent. No matter how much my wolf wanted to.

I closed my eyes and forced the thought from my mind, concentrating on her body working mine.

Her legs tightened around me, and I shifted higher, sliding even deeper into her.

She let out a gasp, arching into me. "More."

With each new thrust she cried out again, and just when I didn't think I would be able to hold on any longer, she wrapped her entire body around me and let out a shuddering moan as she quivered beneath me in her release.

She was so perfect. I stilled, waiting for her to ride the wave. Then as the last shocks rippled through her, I renewed my efforts and was relentless, giving her no reprieve as I thrust hard, burying myself deep inside her, over and over and over again until her cries once again heightened with ecstasy.

"Jace, yes. Oh god yes."

"Say my name again," I demanded.

"Jace." She moaned and clutched her sex around me.

I lost all control then and quickened my pace, hitting just the right spot, both of us crying out as we tumbled over the edge together.

Afterward, careful to not crush her with my

weight, I rolled off her and disappeared into the bathroom to clean up and dispose of the condom. When I returned, I lay on top of the comforter, staring at the open-beam ceiling.

Her breathing had slowed, but I swore I could still hear the thump of her heartbeat filling the small cabin.

It was the connection. Satisfaction mixed with a trace of panic ran through me. It hadn't just been the sex that had made me want to mate with her. *She was the one.*

A ball of happiness filled my chest. I'd found her. The one I was meant to be with forever. Only how could I tell her? How could I convince her to stay in this tiny bayou town out in the middle of nowhere? I needed time. Needed her to stay, needed more afternoons spent like this.

"Jace?"

I didn't turn to look at her. "Yeah?"

She propped herself up on one elbow and stared down at me. "Should I be sorry?"

That got my attention. I turned and nearly cursed when I saw the irritation in those vibrant blue eyes. "No. Of course not. Why?"

She raised one eyebrow. "Because, normally when a guy rolls off a woman like that and says nothing, especially after… Well, it just usually means he wants to get rid of her as soon as possible. But since there's a storm, there's really nowhere for either of us to go."

"No, it's not that. I just…" Son of a bitch. What was I supposed to say? *That after waiting for thirty years, I'd finally found my true mate and that after an hour of fucking our brains out, I'm ready to turn you werewolf and make it forever?* God no.

Skye let out a slow breath and in a quiet, steady voice, said, "If it's all the same to you, I'd rather not do the awkward after-copulation dance. I'm not expecting anything from you, all right? I got caught up in the moment. And to be clear, I'm not sorry. But can we skip whatever explanation you're trying to form. Is that all right with you?"

I sat up and stared her straight in the eye. "We can do whatever you want. But for the record, even if we weren't trapped on this island, I wouldn't be going anywhere after what we just did. And neither would you."

She clamped her mouth shut and studied me.

I smiled at her, twining my fingers through hers. "Lie down with me."

She didn't say anything, so I gently tugged her down, turning her so her back was to my chest as I spooned her naked body.

"I'm sorry," she said so quietly I almost didn't hear her.

"Stop, you have nothing to be sorry for." I wrapped my arm around her waist and brought my hand up to cup her breast, loving the weight of her in my palm.

"I just meant I wasn't trying to be a drama queen."

"I know. It's my fault." I pressed a kiss to her creamy white shoulder. "You rocked my world, and it took a moment for me to recover."

"Oh." She chuckled. "In that case…"

I tightened my grip on her breast and teased the flesh of her neck, stopping at her already rapidly increasing pulse. I tilted my head and whispered, "Later. I think we might both need a rest."

Letting out a contented sigh, she snuggled into me. After a few moments, I felt her limbs go liquid as the tension drained from her.

My heart jolted and I nearly jerked back, not at all accustomed to someone trusting me so much so fast. Instead I tightened my hold, unwilling to let her go. People didn't just fall asleep in the arms of a werewolf. There was an inherent flight response even when they had no idea the man they were with was really a shifter.

Jesus fucking Christ. If I couldn't get her to stay… I forced the thought from my mind. That wasn't an option.

CHAPTER 5

SKYE

I WOKE WITH a jolt, unsure where I was. Then I felt Jace's hand on my hip and the memories came flooding back. His passion, his possession, and the way he'd made every bone in my body go liquid with his attention.

He was Trouble with a capital *T*.

The way he'd captivated me, and the way I'd absolutely surrendered myself to him and had loved every minute of it, was completely unacceptable. I'd been overwhelmed by a man before, and look at where that had gotten me. I couldn't let it happen again just because he'd rocked my world one afternoon in a hidden cabin in the bayou. Wouldn't.

I slid out from under his arm, taking one of the discarded blankets with me. The wooden floor was rough against my bare feet as I padded across the room to the window. Wrapping the blanket around my naked body, I stared out at the now-calm waters.

Everything was so still and quiet. It was as if the world had stopped while we'd holed up in the cabin. I glanced back at Jace. He lay on his stomach, head turned toward me, dead to the world as he slept.

Sunlight streamed over his body, and I found my hand itching for my camera. He was breathtaking, all hard lines and tanned skin offset by the vibrant tattoos covering his arms and shoulder.

Letting the blanket fall to the floor, I peered through the viewfinder and took shot after shot of the beautiful man lying so peacefully in the bed. Moving closer, I zoomed in, focusing on the white wolf inked on his shoulder.

Just after I pressed the button down, his hand snaked out and grasped my wrist. I jerked back, letting out a startled cry.

"What are you doing?" he demanded.

"Sorry." I hastily put the camera down, heat flooding my cheeks. "The light. It was perfect and I—"

"Thought you'd help yourself to taking pictures of a naked man without his permission?" He sat up abruptly, anger clouding his expression.

Crap. I bit my lower lip and grimaced.

"You're right. I'm sorry. I wasn't thinking. Sometimes I get caught up in the art and get carried away."

"Give me the camera." His tone left no room for argument.

Still, I hesitated. There was two days' worth of shots on the memory card. Some incredible ones from just before the storm. If he hit the wrong button and erased them, I'd be heart-broken.

"Skye," he growled.

I closed my eyes and handed him the camera, shame overriding my internal arguments. After a moment of silence, I chanced a glance at him.

He was sitting up in the bed, focused on the viewer, all his earlier anger gone. He turned to look at me. "Why did you take these?"

I leaned down and grabbed the discarded blanket, feeling more exposed than ever before. Covering myself, I shrugged. "It's what I do."

He shook his head, that irritation lighting his eyes again. "No, Skye. I mean why did you take these?" He turned the camera around and showed me one—a close-up of his wolf tattoo. "The ones of me. What do you plan to do with them?"

"Oh." My entire body heated with embarrassment. "Nothing. You were lying there looking so… Well, the rays coming through the window created a nice effect. I couldn't resist capturing the moment." I took the camera from him. "I'll delete them."

His hand closed over mine, gently stopping me. "You don't have to do that."

I stared down at the connection between us.

In that moment, it felt more intimate than anything else we'd done in the past few hours. "Are you sure? I don't want to make you uncomfortable."

He chuckled. "Except for the shots that include a couple of my tattoos, I doubt anyone would even know these are me."

I looked up and smiled. "I'd know."

Heat lit his eyes once more. "No doubt."

I glanced at the shots again. None of them showed his face. Most of them were close-ups of certain areas of his body, the focus less on him and more on the play of light.

"They're very artistic," Jace said with an air of respect.

"Thanks. Does this mean you'll sign a release for me to use them commercially?"

His smile vanished. "That's probably not a

good idea."

"No problem," I said, shaking my head. "I understand. I should've never taken them anyway."

He climbed out of the bed, his lean body graceful in his powerful movements. Reaching out, he tucked a lock of hair behind my ear and bent down, claiming my lips with his own.

I melted into him, letting the blanket once again fall to the floor.

"Uncomfortable isn't exactly the word I'd use to describe the way you make me feel right now," he murmured, one hand cupping my ass while the other trailed lazily down my spine.

"Mmm, I like the sound of that." I wrapped one leg around his hip and moaned when his hardness pressed up against my heat.

The faint rumbling of a motor sounded in

the distance. Neither of us paid any attention to it. Jace ran a trail of kisses over my jawline until he got to my neck, where he scraped his teeth over my pulse.

I gasped, wanting him even more that I had the first time.

He let out a low chuckle and pulled me back toward the bed, but then the engine outside cut off abruptly and Jace froze. Releasing me, he stared hard at the door for a second, his head tilted as if he was listening to something. Abruptly, he strode over to the window. "Get dressed," he ordered. "We have company."

"Here? Now?" I scrambled to find my clothes, which were still discarded on the floor. Hastily I pulled on my still damp bra and panties. And just as I was bent over reaching for my dress, the door crashed open, banging against the wall with a loud thud. Aiden, Jace's brother, strode right in, a hardened expression on his face.

"Sorry to interrupt, but—" He stopped and stared intently at me, his mouth open in a surprised "O." Then his eyes narrowed as he crossed the room and grabbed me by the arm. "Why are you here?" He spit the question out with unmistakable hatred. "What do you want?"

"Aiden!" Jace took two steps and yanked his brother off me. "What are you doing?"

I clutched my dress to the front of my body and gaped at them both. What the hell was going on? Jace's brother had never been anything but friendly toward me before.

Aiden pointed at me. "Look at the tattoo on her hip."

Jace frowned, confusion swimming in his narrowed eyes. "What tattoo?"

"Jesus. You didn't even see it?"

I turned, jutting my hip out so Jace could see the small wolf with the trail of pawprints behind him across my lower back. "What about it?"

Jace let go of his brother and the pair of them stood shoulder to shoulder, glaring at me.

Familiar fear seized me. The same fear that had made me run just two days earlier.

CHAPTER 6

JACE

S HE WAS PART of the Hunters. It was the only explanation for the tattoo. The one I hadn't even noticed because I was too busy shoving my dick between her legs.

Fuck.

"I think you better answer Aiden's question, Skye," I said, fighting the urge to put myself between them to shield her from Aiden's wrath.

Dammit.

She held her head high as she tried to put on a brave front. But she couldn't hide from me. Her fear was so strong I could smell it. All of my instincts were telling me to soothe her. To protect her from the shitstorm that would follow once the pack found out.

Frustration coiled in my gut and filled me up, clouding everything else. My mate was one of them.

I closed my hand over the back of the chair, gripping so hard the wood actually splintered under my fingers.

Her gaze latched onto my white knuckles. The sour stench of her fear intensified, followed by an earthy scent, indicating a sheer will of determination. She stared me straight in the eye. "I swear, I only came out here for a photo shoot. Nothing else. I don't know what my tattoo has to do with anything. It's just a tattoo."

"You expect me to believe that, Skye? Is that why your boyfriend, who has a similar piece-of-shit tattoo on his shoulder, is back at the bar demanding to know where you are? Should I haul you back there and let you explain you've been fucking my brother?" The disdain dripping from Aiden's words was enough to shame even the most virtuous person.

A flush claimed her entire body, turning the swell of her breasts rosy pink. My body reacted involuntarily, and I had to stifle a groan.

"For fuck's sake, Jace. Get yourself under control," Aiden said in a harsh whisper.

"Lannister is here?" Her voice shook a bit as she clutched her throat.

"Lannister Clark?" I blurted, all rational thought fleeing. He was one of the leaders for the Southern chapter of the Hunters. It was true. She was one of them. My blood ran cold and a dull pain throbbed in my chest. "That's who your boyfriend is?"

"Was." She averted her gaze, barely able to look at me.

It was clear by her reaction that she knew there was bad blood between us. If she'd been living with Clark, she had to know he'd been the driving force behind trying to steal our land. But did she know why? She had that damned tattoo. The Southern Hunter's symbol with wolf prints in the middle—only hers was slightly different. She had a wolf, too. None of the others did. Not that I'd ever seen, anyway. It didn't add up.

"I think we better get back to the bar," I said, ice in my tone.

"What? No." Skye shook her head, panic

flashing through her eyes. "I can't. Not while he's there."

"Afraid he'll find out you've whored your-self out to get to Jace?" Aiden said with a sneer.

"Hey!" Skye yelled at him before I managed to say anything. As blindsided as I was by the situation, I still wasn't okay with anyone talking to her that way. For better or worse, I couldn't forget she was my mate.

"I already said he *was* my boyfriend, as in no longer. And I don't appreciate the implica-tion that I did anything wrong or that it's indecent or immoral for two consenting adults to sleep together. What I do with my body is my business. And your brother over there, well, he certainly wasn't protesting."

She pulled the dress over her head. Glaring at both of us, she zipped up the back and slipped her feet back into her low-heeled shoes. "Now, I've already said I won't see Lannister. The last time… Let's just say it didn't end well." She focused on me. "I'm sorry. I know he's been a first-class asshole to your family. And honestly, it's one of the reasons I left him. I just found out a few months ago. I swear I had nothing to do with the lawsuit. I should've told you. I know that. But I didn't intend on this happening. All I wanted was a few days away until I figured out where I was going to go. I never dreamed he'd show up here."

Her tone was so earnest it was easy to believe her. But I couldn't take any chances. The risks were too high. "You're right. You should've told me."

"I'm sorry." Tears shone in her eyes, but she blinked them back. "I really am. But please don't take me back there. Would you mind if I stayed here until he's gone?"

Aiden snorted with disbelief. "That's not going to happen."

"Aiden, can you give us a moment?" I nodded toward Skye.

"No. We have to get back. There's been a…" He glanced at Skye, shooting her a look of irritation. "A development in that problem we've been having. It's urgent. And judging by what I've found here, I think it's pretty obvious you've been played."

"I have no idea what you're talking about." Skye crossed her arms over her chest as her expression went flat, almost uncaring. She was doing her best to mask her feelings. But she couldn't hide them from me. Despite her obvious determination to appear strong, fear had taken over, mixed with something that smelled like confusion.

Was it possible she really didn't know what Lannister had been up to besides the lawsuit? That she wasn't part of the Hunters and didn't know we were shifters? A small twinge of hope spread like wildfire through my gut. The Southern Hunters were a small, paranoid group whose only mission in life seemed to be stamping out the packs due to their own prejudices. But they also kept our secret because they wanted our land. Better to take it from us than other poachers or worse—the government.

"Where did you get the tattoo?" I asked her.

"Talk about it on the boat," Aiden said. "We have to go." He stomped out of the cabin, leaving the door wide open.

"Not that it's any of your business, but I got

it at a shop in New Orleans. Lannister has the prints and I thought they were interesting. He'd wanted me to get them for a while and finally I did. But when he saw the wolf, he lost it, told me I'd disfigured myself and... Well, things didn't last long after that." Skye moved over to the door. "As it just so happens, wolves mean something to me. And if you have a problem with it, you can go to hell." She whirled and ran out of the house toward the airboat.

I stared after her for a minute, then followed, locking the door behind me. Aiden had already taken off in the little fishing boat, and Skye was sitting in the front row of the airboat, steadfastly not looking at me. Her camera was clutched in her lap as if she were holding on to it for dear life.

I jumped into the rear of the boat and sat in

the driver's seat. Before doing anything else, I sucked in a breath and asked, "Why wolves?"

Silence.

I debated waiting her out. I had her in the middle of the bayou. I could effectively hold her captive until she answered my questions, but Aiden's message meant I didn't have that kind of time. Lannister and his bullshit had only intensified after they'd lost a lawsuit to force us off our land. And five days ago he had come around wielding his rifle. After he'd fired off a shot and hit Luc in the arm, he'd lost not only his rifle but also the use of his left hand after I got done with him.

The only problem was he'd escaped before we'd decided what to do with him. Chances were high that's why Lannister was back. Unless he'd been searching for Skye. It wouldn't have been hard to tell where she was considering her Jeep was in the bar parking lot.

Either way, I couldn't take her back there. She'd have to wait somewhere safe until we got rid of Lannister. Whether she'd been telling me the truth about what she knew or not, it didn't matter to me. She'd said they broke up, and I believed her. And she was mine now. Lannister wouldn't even get a chance to set eyes on her.

I stared at the back of her head, swallowing my frustration. "Fine. Don't tell me why you got the tattoo. But you will eventually." I fired up the motor. Ten minutes later, I pulled the boat up to a dock next to a white cottage.

"Where are we?" Skye asked.

I tied the boat up and held my hand out to her.

She ignored me and jumped out, stumbling

when the dock rocked under her weight.

I reached out, steadying her.

"Let go." She shrugged me off, scowling at me.

It was almost amusing how her temper had risen on the short ride. Though I had to admit I preferred her being pissed off as opposed to frightened. Backbone was needed around these parts.

She glanced around. "How do I get to my car?"

"You don't. Not yet anyway. I'm leaving you here at Luc's place. Rayna will look after you until I get back."

"Do I have a choice?" she asked, a look of resignation on her face.

I shook my head. "It's safer for you here."

She sighed. "Probably. Who are Rayna and

Luc?"

"Luc is my other brother and Rayna is a friend of the family. I'll be back later tonight to pick you up. In the meantime, listen to Rayna. She—"

Skye cut me off with a humorless laugh. "Listen to Rayna? Someone I don't even know who probably thinks I'm a traitor? Sure. After the way you and your brother just treated me, I'm certain she's going to be the epitome of hospitality." Fire burned in those sapphire-blue eyes, and I felt a smile start to tug at my lips. Earlier she'd been all sex and passion. Now she was fierce and not taking shit from anyone. It was enough to make me want her all over again.

I suppressed the urge to smile and nodded solemnly. "You're right. We were dicks. But we have things to talk about, and right now I have to go deal with this problem. Will you wait with Rayna? I'll make sure she keeps her attitude in check."

She sucked in a breath, glanced at the dirt road and back at me. Sighing, she shrugged. "What else am I going to do? Walk?"

It was about five miles back to the bar through the woods, ten by road. There was no way she'd make it there on foot before nightfall without getting lost. "I'd rather you didn't."

She rolled her eyes, a twinge of a smile tugging at her lips. "After that gator almost took my head off today? No thanks."

The tightening in my gut eased. "I'll be back in a few hours."

"You better." She turned on her heel and strode up the cabin's steps.

I watched her for a second, my inner wolf

rising to the surface.

Mine.

"You coming?" she asked.

I shook off the beginning stages of the shift and joined her on the porch. Holding the door open, I waved her in. "Rayna?"

The pretty brunette appeared from the back of the house, dressed in cutoffs and a skintight tank top. "Jace?" She cut a glance at Skye. "Who's this?"

"I'm the dangerous outsider," Skye said as she flopped down into a red leather chair. "And you're my babysitter."

Rayna lifted a dark eyebrow and gave me a dubious look. "Seriously?"

"We have a problem back at the bar. I just need the two of you to sit tight until we take care of it."

Rayna stiffened. "Where's Luc?"

She understood immediately. While Rayna wasn't a wolf herself, she'd practically grown up with Luc and knew everything about our pack. "Last time I saw him, he was headed to the bank. I'm not sure. I've got to go."

She nodded and followed me out the door. "Make 'em pay, Jace."

"I plan on it." I waved at the house. "You should know she used to date Lannister, but I'm unclear what she knows and what she doesn't. So be careful what you say to her, all right?"

Rayna crossed her arms over her chest. "Lannister? You can't be serious?"

"Afraid so."

"Jesus, Jace." She pushed her dark hair off her forehead and blew out a breath. "And you want me to keep her here? That's asking a lot, don't you think?"

"It is, but I don't really have any other choice." I lowered my voice. "Look, she's afraid of him. And I'm sure as hell not going to let her get anywhere near that asshole."

Rayna narrowed her eyes. "Do you have something going with this girl?"

I focused on the thick tree line, deliberately avoiding the question.

"Son of a…" she muttered. "You know that could all be an act. She could be reporting back to him."

I ground my teeth together, stifling a growl of frustration. "Of course I know that, but my wolf says otherwise."

"Well, then. That's all we need to know then isn't it," she said dryly.

"Dammit, Ray. You know how this works. You're going to have to trust me."

"If you say so."

"I do. Now please keep an eye on her until I get back." Without waiting for her answer, I took off in a sprint toward the woods. The moment I hit the tree line, I quickly divested myself of my clothes, tossed them aside, and leaped forward, my bones creaking with the shift.

CHAPTER 7

SKYE

RAYNA CHARGED BACK into the house, ranting something about inconsiderate assholes. She took one look at me and disappeared into the other room. When she came out, she had a small handgun stuffed into the waistband of her jeans.

"Whoa!" She had an actual gun. Oh my God. Jesus. Fighting off a panic attack, I held my hands up. "You don't need that. I swear, I'm nobody. I have no idea what's going on. I'm just a photographer. I came down here for bayou and wildlife shots. Not to get in the middle of some backcountry war."

"Relax," Rayna said as she stared out the window. "It's not because of you. It's so I can be prepared in case Lannister shows up here again."

"Again? He's been here before?" My heart thudded in my chest. What in the hell had I walked into? People always said to be careful when you go into the bayou. But I knew this small town. Had figured it would be the last place Lannister would look for me, especially since I'd been scheduled to do a shoot in Tennessee this weekend. There was no reason for me to be here other than I had just wanted to be.

Rayna nodded. "Five days ago. He put a bullet hole in Luc's arm too."

"He did what? Why?" Five days ago had been the start of our epic showdown. It was right after Lannister had shown up with his left hand wrapped in thick gauze after having been gone for hours. He'd strode in smelling like two-day-old fish and had refused to tell me what happened to him. He'd also ordered me to cook him dinner, bathe him, and then give him a blow job when I was done.

I'd responded by throwing a glass candlestick at his head. My only regret was that I'd nicked the side of his face instead of bashing it in.

"You do know about the lawsuit, right? I mean, being his girlfriend and all, I guess you'd have to."

"Ex-girlfriend. And all I know about the lawsuit is he claimed his great-great-grandfather had mineral rights to the land and he'd been trying to make a claim or something."

Rayna snorted her disbelief. "Is that what he told you? Bastard. The real story is he's trying to run the Riveauxs out of town because of a… ah, personal grudge. His claim is utterly bogus, but he spent months filing new motions with the lawsuit, hoping it would bankrupt them."

How many times had I heard of a delay with the court date? And every time Lannister had said the judge had postponed the supposedly simple hearing. God. I'd been so naïve. My stomach turned at having spent the past year with someone I obviously hadn't known at all. In the beginning, he'd been careful, sweet, attentive. It'd only been the last few months that his true nature had started to show. Selfish.

Petty. And mean.

Tears burned the back of my eyes, but I blinked them back. Not because I cared about him in any way, but because I was humiliated. He'd indirectly made me a party to his heinous actions. "That's awful. All of it."

Rayna paced silently over the rough wood floors in her bare feet. "Yep. Real piece of shit that one."

She didn't have to convince me. As far as I was concerned, he deserved to be in prison. I fingered the still-tender bruise on the right side of my head. It was the work of Lannister after I'd told him I was leaving three days ago. And more than anything, I regretted not going to the hospital and filing the police report. But there was nothing the hospital could do, and all I'd wanted was to get out of town.

I couldn't take sitting down anymore. The idea that I was stranded in the bayou with a stranger, that whatever was going on had prompted her to pack a gun, the scene back at the bayou shack with Aiden and Jace. It was too much. It was either ask questions or run screaming from the house. Running almost won out. Instead, I got up and joined Rayna by the window. "See anything?"

She shook her head. "Nope. Everything's quiet."

"That's good, right?" I scanned the area and focused on the airboat. I hadn't realized Jace had left it.

"Yes and no. Good that the Hun—uh, good that the problem hasn't found its way here. Not so good that we have no idea what's going on back at the bar."

I couldn't agree more. I had half a mind to steal the airboat and head back there to kick Lannister in the balls. The bastard. But if I was honest, it was because I wanted to be where Jace was. Make sure he was okay. "Rayna?"

"Yeah?"

"Can you tell me why my tattoo caused such an uproar when Aiden saw it? I mean, he really lost it. Then Jace got all moody and intense."

She raised her hand to her throat and appeared to contemplate how much she wanted to say. Then she cast her gaze down the length of my body and back up again. "Can I see it?"

I shrugged. "I guess. It's just a wolf and some pawprints."

"Show me." Her tone was earnest.

Unzipping my dress, I turned my back to

her. I slipped my arms out of the straps and held the bodice against my chest.

Rayna whistled. "No wonder they freaked out."

I pulled my dress back on, suddenly feeling too exposed. "Why?"

"Because it's very close to the ones Lannister and his minions have. It's not exactly the same, though. The ones I've seen don't actually have a wolf. But you know that already, right?"

"Yeah. Lannister just has the prints."

"He'd probably stab himself in the eye first before he'd get an actual wolf. But the prints, they're the same. They signify tracking."

"As in tracking wolves? To do what? Hunt them?" I asked, horrified.

She sucked in a breath. "Yes. That's exactly what it means."

"Mine don't. They're the wolf's pawprints. You know, as if I'm walking with the wolf. Not tracking, and certainly never hunting." I clenched my jaw in defiance. "Wolves are majestic. Trackers are… Oh my God. Does that mean Lannister's a tracker? Has he been out here hunting the wolves?"

She stilled and studied me, her shoulders tense.

"It's true then," I said, gutted.

"I didn't even answer."

"You didn't have to. It's written all over your face."

She pushed her hair back off her forehead and paced near the door. "It's not something we usually talk about around here."

"You should. Hunting wolves is uncon-scionable. And the fact that I have a tattoo that is in any way associated with his kind makes me ill." I choked out a humorless laugh. "You know, he told me the symbol meant serenity. I liked it, so I had it added when I got my wolf. I've been wanting a wolf for years."

Rayna stopped in front of me and, voice soft, asked, "Why a wolf?"

I shrugged. "I have this thing where I dream about wolves. They're majestic, you know? I guess I always thought of them as my spirit animal."

Rayna let out a low whistle and stared at me with interest. "That explains a lot."

I shook my head, not really understanding what she was trying to say. "Explains what?"

"Why Jace is drawn to you."

How could she know that? Speculation because I'd spent the afternoon with him? Sure, we'd known each other for a while, but it had been months since I'd been out this way. Did he talk about me with her? My stomach did a little flip at the thought. But then I shut it down. I was letting my imagination get away from me. She had to be talking about what happened this afternoon. And honestly, how many single men would turn down no-strings-attached sex? Especially when they were stranded due to a storm. None. "If you say so."

She chuckled. "I think we're going to be seeing a lot of each other from now on."

"Not if Aiden has his way."

She patted my arm. "Don't worry about him. He'll come around."

"So you don't think I'm some criminal sent here by my gang to set Jace up for something?"

"Nope." She gave me a small smile. "Listen.

That tattoo you have? The symbol in the tracks means silence. As in silence the packs. The wolf packs around here. Some people think they should be rounded up and contained. And still others think they should be eliminated altogether. That's why Aiden thought you were one of them. But unless my instincts are way the fuck off, you just got mixed up with the wrong people."

"You can say that again," I muttered.

She gave me a sympathetic smile. "Sounds like you didn't need our help to figure that one out."

"You're not wrong. Lannister can be charming and talks a good game, but when he's being himself and has all his social guards down, he's an asshole of epic proportions. I left him because of his jealousy issues, among other things. I never knew about his role in trying to hunt the wolves. It makes sense he never let me in on that dirty little secret though. In my circles, it's well-known I have a love for the animals. A lot of my art features them."

"Is that why you're here then? To get pictures of the wolves?" There was weariness in her tone now.

I nodded. "Yes. And while I was here I was going to get bayou shots, and in a few days, a couple of my model friends are coming down to do a shoot with me. I'm really here just to work."

"No one's going to like that."

"Why?" I asked.

"You'll see."

CHAPTER 8

JACE

I STOOD IN front of the bar, Aiden and Luc flanking me on either side. Skye's ex, the jackass known as Lannister, leaned against his truck, holding his rifle in one hand and a hunting knife in the other. A cigarette dangled from his lips as he sneered at us.

"I'm here to collect payment for this." He held up his bandaged hand, the one I'd all but ripped off his arm five days ago. "But it appears you have something else of mine to return as well." He jerked his head toward Skye's Jeep parked in front of the bar. "Where's that bitch hiding?"

The urge to rip his throat out sent my wolf straight to the surface. My muscles bunched with the impulse to shift, and if it hadn't been for Luc stepping forward with his shotgun, I might have.

My youngest brother positioned the weapon against his uninjured shoulder and aimed. "Our patrons are none of your concern. Now, you can leave peacefully or you can take your chances with the smoking end of this gun."

"You're not going to shoot anyone, Riveaux." Lannister sneered. "You can't even put a bullet in a turkey during hunting season."

"Good thing I'm aiming at a jackass instead then, isn't it?"

Lannister's muscles flexed as he gripped his

weapons harder, and his face turned red with irritation. "Keep it up, Riveaux, and I'll put a hole in the other arm."

I'd had enough. Stepping beside Luc, I crossed my arms over my chest. "Keep it up, Lannister, and you'll lose that other hand."

The tall man's eyes narrowed with undeniable hatred. "You can go to hell."

"You first," Luc said and squeezed the trigger of the shotgun.

The loud boom sent Lannister diving toward his bright red Ford F-150 as the buckshot sailed high into the air toward the uninhabited swamp.

Aiden laughed. "Chickenshit."

"Get off our property or I'm calling the sheriff," I said.

Lannister's face scrunched up with pure

venom. "Go ahead. I look forward to pressing charges for the mauling that happened here last week, *wolf.*"

For a fleeting moment I had an image of killing him with my bare hands and feeding him to Betsy for dinner. "No one around here is going to believe your lies."

"No?" He held up a smartphone. "My buddy is an amateur videographer. Turns out he recorded our... interaction last week." He threw the phone at my feet. "Go ahead, check it out."

"Get it," I said to Aiden, not taking my eyes off the Hunter.

Aiden grunted and retrieved the phone. A moment later he muttered, "Fucking cocksucker."

"What's on it?" I asked, noting Lannister's

smug, shit-eating grin.

"He cut the part when the bastard shot Luc."

"No surprise there," I said.

"It starts with the weasel offering to leave us alone for good in exchange for a modest settlement in addition to a public acknowledgment that his grandfather was the original landowner. Then it cuts to you shifting into wolf form just before you maul him."

Fuck.

If the tape was analyzed, there wouldn't be any evidence of splicing because events had happened just like that. Only Lannister had made that offer moments *after* he'd shot Luc and threatened to go after Rayna. We'd all known the offer had been bullshit, not that we'd have taken him up on it. The lawsuit had already been thrown out.

I took a step forward and clutched the support beam on the porch. Gritting my teeth, I asked, "What exactly do you want from us this time, Lannister?"

His evil smile widened. "Just a contract that says you'll pay me fifty grand a year for land rights, and in exchange I'll destroy the video."

"He's out of his fucking mind," Aiden said behind me.

"How much are your lives worth to you, boys?" Lannister pulled an envelope from his back pocket and waved it at us.

"We're not signing anything," Luc chimed in. "You can take your contract and go fuck yourself with it."

"I would, but I have Skye for that. Sign the contract, hand over my fiancée, and this can all go away."

My vision clouded and a dull roar filled my ears. I was full of pure, unadulterated rage, the kind that filled every space in my brain and drowned out everything else. Everything except that small voice that held me back from shifting. Not here. Not in front of the bar where humans could see. The centuries-old rule was so ingrained in my psyche I was certain it was the only thing that kept me in human form. Because anywhere else, I'd already have my jaws around the bastard's neck.

Jumping off the porch, I was faintly aware of voices shouting behind me, but I ignored the calls as I stalked forward, heading straight for Lannister. By the time I was done with him, it'd be months before he could try to blackmail anyone again.

"Hold it right there, Riveaux," Lannister said, pointing his gun to the right of me.

"Or what? You're going to shoot—" The faint smell of citrus hit me, and memories from the afternoon flooded my mind. I turned abruptly. "Skye? What are you doing here?"

"We heard gun shots," she said angrily, glaring at Lannister. "We couldn't just sit around and wait to see if you guys were bleeding out, now could we?"

"You shouldn't be here." I took a step to the right, putting myself between her and Lannister's gun. That asshole had been aiming at her, not Aiden or Luc. To him I said, "Is that how you keep your women in line? By force?"

"Jace," Skye said, tugging my arm, "Come on. He's not worth it.

But I was planted and didn't budge.

Lannister gave me a half shrug and leered at Skye over my shoulder. "If she's being a cunt, like that traitorous bitch you're protecting, then yeah."

A growl rippled from the back of my throat. "Don't ever talk about Skye that way."

"What are you going to do, wolf, shift right in front of her?"

Skye let out a surprised gasp. A ball of frustration formed in the pit of my stomach. This was not how she was supposed to learn about my shifter side.

"Go ahead, tell her all about how you nearly ripped my hand off earlier this week in a fit of animal rage. Let your new toy in on your secret and see how long she sticks around."

"Shut up, Lannister," Skye spat. "You shot his brother. And you've been fucking around with their livelihood for months. And for what? Because you're afraid of them?"

Lannister's eyes turned almost black as his body tensed with what could only be called hatred. "I'm not afraid of anyone. Least of all these mutant freaks of nature."

"That's enough," I said, my tone low and dangerous. "I suggest you put the gun down, get back in your truck, and get out of here before someone gets hurt."

"You afraid your new whore is going to interfere when I blow your hand off? Well, don't worry. I know how to tame her," Lannister said with an evil laugh as he lunged for her.

That control I'd steadfastly held to snapped. The shift took over, my bones shrinking and elongating into the massive four-legged creature I was born to be. Without hesitating I leaped, my jaws catching Lannister around the neck as I tackled him to the asphalt.

His screams covered the clatter of his weapons hitting the ground behind us as well as the shouts of my packmates ordering me to stand down. But that wasn't going to happen. My inner wolf had to get him as far from Skye as possible. Lannister wasn't allowed to touch her. Not anymore. Not now that I knew she was mine.

Ignoring everyone around me, I sank my fangs into his neck and tugged, dragging him across the parking lot toward the property line.

"Jace!" Skye's feminine voice pierced all the chaos around me and I paused, cocking an ear to listen to what she had to say.

"Stop. It's not worth killing him over. The sheriff is on his way. Please, let him go and we'll press charges. I'll press charges for what he did to me three days ago."

Growling, I tightened my hold and shook my head slightly, tasting the spray of warm blood on my tongue, and continued toward the trees. If he'd laid a hand on Skye, he deserved whatever he got.

"Don't." Skye pressed her hand to my neck, stopping me mid-step. "If you kill him, it'll only draw more questions to your pack."

I dropped the limp man and turned my head to stare at her, astonished. She was talking as if she knew all about us. Like she was okay with it and wanted to be sure we were kept safe. My heart swelled with pleasure. Forgetting Lannister, I called on the shift again.

Skye let out a startled laugh and then sobered as I stood naked before her, my gaze locked on hers.

"You know?" I asked.

She licked her lips and nodded. "I think I kind of always knew. Years ago when I first came out here, I saw a small pack. They were so intelligent. Appeared to just belong here as if they owned the place. It's exactly the same vibe I get from you. It was… magical."

I smiled and brushed my knuckles over her cheek. "That was me, Aiden, and a few of our distant cousins."

"You remember." Pleasure swam in her blue gaze.

"Of course I do. You came back four times that year."

She grinned up at me. "And you made sure I saw you each time."

I chuckled. "Well, I wanted you to get what

you came for." Sobering, I said, "But a few months after that last time you saw us, a small group of Hunters spotted us and nearly killed one of our cousins. Our public appearances stopped that day."

Her eyes clouded with outrage and she opened her mouth to respond, but movement drew my attention just before Lannister swung his arm out and caught me in the back of the knee, sending me sprawling to the ground with an "Oomph."

He scrambled to his feet and loomed over me, his booted foot pressed into my neck. "Sorry to interrupt memory lane, but we have business to attend to." He threw the papers he'd been holding earlier down on the ground near my face. "Sign it or I'm going to break your fucking neck and call it self-defense. I have the puncture wounds to prove it."

Cursing myself for being an idiot, I scented the air and caught the faint trace of my brothers. They'd shifted as well. It wasn't a surprise. When one of us was out of control it usually triggered the shift in the others. They were circling, looking for an opening. If I could stall, it would give them an opportunity to strike.

"That's enough!" Skye cried.

"Skye, no. Stay out of this."

Lannister laughed. "She never could mind her own business."

"Neither can I," Rayna said, followed by the double pump of a shotgun. "Move off my friend, or I'll blow your head off."

A smile tugged at my lips. Damn, she really was one of us.

From my vantage point on the ground I saw

Lannister raise his hands slowly.

"Move your foot away from his neck," Skye added, her fists clenched as she stood next to Rayna.

He sneered at her but reluctantly backed up, putting at least a foot between us.

"That's good," Rayna said. "Now move over there." She jerked the gun, indicating he should move to stand in the middle of the near-empty parking lot.

"Bitch."

"That's right. But you're still going to do as I say or else you're going to be in a world of pain in about two seconds."

Grumbling something about making her pay, he kicked some lose gravel in my direction and walked stiffly to the spot she'd indicated.

"Here." Skye tossed me my pants.

I grabbed them and even though they were torn in multiple spots, I tugged them on.

"Now what?" Lannister asked. "Is this where you knock me out and feed me to the gators? Because you should know at least half a dozen people know where I am right now."

"You're an idiot," Skye said, stalking up to him.

"Skye, no," I grabbed her hand and tugged her back. "Don't."

She put her other hand up in a stop motion. "Trust me. I have this."

Aiden and Luc, still in their wolf form, closed in around us, and Rayna still had the shotgun trained on him. I squeezed Skye's hand and then let go. "Fine, but if he moves even an inch, I'm taking him out."

She sent Lannister a cold smile. "Fine by me."

CHAPTER 9

SKYE

"WHAT DO YOU want, Skye? Because you have to know by now I'm not letting you back in my house." Lannister spat, barely missing my foot.

I gave him a flat stare, ignoring his effort to taunt me. "This is what's going to happen. You're going to leave the Riveauxs alone. No more lawsuits, no more showing up here, no more blackmail. And you're going to sign paperwork that says you don't have any interest in their land, and as far as you know there is no evidence of any claim."

"Why would I do that?" His condescending smirk made me want to punch him in the gut.

"Because if you don't, I'm going to overnight some documents I happened to find in your desk when I was packing up my things a few days ago to the nearest DEA office."

His mouth fell open in shock, followed quickly by a hardening of his eyes. "You were going through my things?"

"Good thing, too. It's coming in handy right about now." I'd been looking for my birth certificate when I'd come across two sets of books for his one-man-show accounting business. Turns out Lannister was laundering marijuana money through his LLC. "How'd you like a nice long stay in the state pen?"

"You can't prove anything," he said, but his

voice shook and I knew I had him.

"Of course I can. You don't think I left without evidence, do you? Especially after you slammed my head into the wall."

"He did what?" Jace asked, closing the distance between us.

I placed a hand on his arm, hoping the connection would keep him from ripping Lannister's guts out. "We got into it and instead of walking away, Lannister thought I could use some sense knocked into me. But I'm fine, really."

"And you didn't press charges?"

I shook my head. "I should have, but it was then I decided to take the books just in case I needed leverage. Looks like I was right." I turned to Lannister. "So, do we have a deal?"

He was silent for a long moment.

"Would you prefer to be shot in the knee?" Rayna asked sweetly.

He glared at her. Then he closed his eyes and said, "Fine. I'll sign the document."

"Good." Relief washed through my body.

"But I want those books back," he said.

I shook my head. "No. You have the wolf video, we have the cooked books. There's no way for either of us to know if the other has a copy. So let's just assume we do. This way both parties have an incentive to keep the other's secret."

Rayna let out a low whistle. "Wow, nice bargaining."

"You can say that again," Jace said from behind me.

"Well?" I asked Lannister.

He let out a long sigh. "Fine. Deal."

I turned to Jace and grinned. "Looks like you owe me one."

His lips twitched. "Just one?"

"Okay, maybe two."

He chuckled. "I think I can handle that."

TWO HOURS LATER, after documents had been signed and we'd watched Lannister drive off the Riveaux property for hopefully the last time, I sat in Jace's living room, which looked remarkably like the shack we'd spent the afternoon in. Only his place was four rooms instead of one and it wasn't on an island.

"Come here." He stood in front of me where I was curled into one of the black leather chairs and held a hand out to me. "Sit with me on the couch."

Jace pulled me up and then positioned us on the matching couch so he was leaning against the arm and I was leaning against him. He wrapped his arms around me, resting them on my stomach. "I have a few things to tell you."

"I suppose you do," I said, content to just be held.

"I haven't… Well, I've only ever told one other person outside the pack about my shifter abilities."

"Grace?" I guessed.

He nodded.

I'd met her once or twice. They'd dated for a long time, but about a year ago they'd broken up. "What happened? She just decided she couldn't deal with it?"

"Sort of." He cleared his throat. "She was fine with the shifter part. It was the other stuff she had problems with."

I glanced back at him. "What other stuff? The secrecy? Surely she understood the dangers?" I couldn't imagine ever leaving the beautiful creature sitting behind me. The wolf was majestic of course, but so was the man.

"It was the mating." He let the words hang in the air for a moment.

I squeezed his fingers in encouragement. "I don't know what that is."

"Sorry. I know you don't." He began tracing my shoulder with his knuckles. "Every year we, the wolves, have from March first until Beltane to take a mate. To make them one of the pack. If we miss the window, we have to wait. And with our numbers so low, there's pressure on all of us to mate. It was too much for her."

I jerked up and twisted to look him in the eye. "Mate? Are you saying you asked her to have a child with you before she was ready?"

"No!" He shook his head. "When one takes a mate, he hopes to build the family, but that's not all it's for. Mates strengthen the pack. Build numbers. But also make us stronger. They are necessary for survival. If you get lucky, you find your true mate, like a soul mate, but most of us don't. We find someone we admire and respect to mate with.

"Was Grace your true mate?" I asked, pain already filling my heart. I knew I wanted him, every part of him, but if he had a soul mate out there he was pining for, I couldn't stay. Couldn't be his lover knowing he wanted someone else.

His chest shook with a silent laugh. "God no, Skye. You are."

I bolted upright and sat facing him, finding a touch of vulnerability and anxiousness in his expression. "What?"

"I knew it this afternoon when we made love. Well, that first touch, really. You tame my wolf with your mere presence and bring him out with your heated kisses. I know it's a lot to take in, but after today, I thought you had a right to know."

"But what does it mean?" I asked, my heart thudding against my rib cage.

Both of his hands ran up and down my sides, barely grazing the curve of my breasts. "It means that I want to mark you with my bite, turn you were, and make you part of my pack. I know it's fast, but we still have a month or so of mating season before I need an answer."

Shock dumbfounded me, my mind reeling. He wanted to turn me. Make me his forever.

Yes. That voice that lived in the back of my head shouted at me. And everything tingled as my heart clenched. I wanted him too. Wanted to be part of the pack. More than anything.

"When can we do it?" I asked.

He looked at me in surprise. "When?"

I laced my fingers in his. "Yeah, when? And how? I'm in. All in."

When the confusion didn't dissipate, I added in a soft tone, "Don't you know I've been half in love with you since the first day I came out here?"

He shook his head. "No. I didn't know that."

I shrugged. "Our timing was off. You had

Grace. Then I was with… Well, I was unavaila-ble. It happens. Doesn't mean I didn't want you."

His hand tightened on my hip. "I always wanted you, too."

"Good. Then we'll be compatible." I leaned in and pressed my lips to his, letting him know the feeling was mutual.

"Skye?" he said against my lips.

"Hmm?"

"There's more."

"Okay," I said between kisses.

Placing both his hands on my shoulders, he eased me back so he could make eye contact. "To form the mating bond, I have to bite you."

"Okay. In wolf form?" That sounded slight-ly terrifying, but it wasn't going to make me back down. I wanted this too much.

"No, love," he said with a tiny smile. "While we're having sex."

It shouldn't have, but those words sent a shiver of desire to all the right places. "Seriously?"

He nodded. "Yep."

I lowered my gaze back to his lips. "Then we better get busy, because I want to see what I look like in wolf form."

He stared at me in awe. "You're serious."

"Damn straight I'm serious. Wolves are my thing. Or didn't you notice I have one tattooed on my hip?"

"Oh, I noticed all right." Then, without another word, he stood and picked me up, carrying me to the bedroom.

He set me on my feet, and for the second time that day, watched me step out of my clothes. When I was naked before him, he hastily discarded his own. But before he touched me, he asked, "You're sure? I'd feel better if you took some time to think it over."

I eyed his magnificent erection and shook my head. "Less thinking, more fucking."

He closed his eyes, sucking in a breath, and when he opened them, they were so full of desire my knees nearly buckled from anticipation. "You're wet already."

"How can you tell?" I asked. "You haven't even touched me yet."

"I'm were; I can tell."

"Oh." I had a fleeting thought that I should be embarrassed, but his bluntness only turned me on more.

"Lie down on the bed."

I did as I was told.

"Spread your legs."

Once again I obeyed, but I also crooked a finger, coaxing him to join me.

He stood over the bed, gazing at me, his muscles quivering in anticipation.

"Jace?"

"Yeah?"

"If you don't take me soon, I'm going to take your dick in my mouth and torture you until you beg me to finish you off."

He raised both eyebrows and cast his gaze down the length of my body, stopping only when he focused on my sex. "Tempting, but I have other plans."

Then he crawled over me and buried his face between my legs. His tongue was so insistent, so practiced, so fucking perfect, that just as he got started, my muscles clenched, an orgasm shaking me to the core. I'd come harder and faster than ever before. "Jesus," I mumbled.

Jace chuckled against my thigh, and then before I even had a chance to take a breath, he plunged into me, his shaft filling me so completely I thought I'd die of pleasure.

"You feel so good," I said.

"Not as good as you do," he gasped out. "So hot. So tight. So fucking willing."

I answered by tightening my legs around his hips and rocking up to meet his thrusts. It didn't take long for the tension to build, and suddenly we were both gasping, barely holding on before losing ourselves to one another.

"Do it," I ordered, clutching his ass with both hands. "Bite me. Make me yours. Make me your mate."

"Oh, God," Jace cried, and with a growl of

pure pleasure, he sank his teeth into my shoulder.

My entire body shuddered in pleasure as another orgasm crashed through me and took him over the edge with me.

I woke the next morning to Jace trailing kisses down the back of my neck. Pressing my hand to my forehead, I let out a small moan of pain.

"Hey." Jace rose up on one elbow, concern creasing his brow. "Are you all right?"

"I don't know." I pulled myself up and assessed the situation. The bite on my shoulder had all but healed already, but there was a slight throbbing in my temple. "I think I have a minor headache."

A slow grin spread over Jace's features. "I can help with that."

"I bet."

He reached over to his night table, grabbed a bottled water and some aspirin. "Here."

"Is it weird I'm strangely disappointed by this?" I asked him, staring at the aspirin bottle. "I was expecting something a little more… physical."

Heat lit his dark gaze. "That can be arranged."

Just the thought of his lips and fingers on me sent my pulse racing and my sensitive places throbbing. The headache vanished and a hunger that had nothing to do with food took over. I placed the water and pills back on his nightstand and then straddled him. "I want you. All of you, *mate.*"

"Fuck," he said on a groan. "I can't believe how sexy it is when you say that."

"Show me."

He ran his hand up my inner thigh while nuzzling my shoulder where he'd bitten me the night before. Lightning bolts of desire rippled through me.

"I hope you didn't have plans today," Jace said.

I shook my head. "My only plan now is to be with you."

He pulled back slightly, brushed a whisper of a kiss over my lips, and said, "Mine. Forever."

And I was. Utterly and completely his. Mated for life.

Sign up for Kenzie's newsletter at www. kenziecox.com to be notified of new releases. Do you prefer text messages? Sign up for text alerts! Just text SHIFTERSROCK to 24587 to register.

Book List:

Wolves of the Rising Sun

Jace

Aiden

Luc

Craved

Silas

Darien

Wren

.

Printed in Great Britain
by Amazon

70024993R00090